The Snow Princess

Ruth Sanderson

LITTLE, BROWN AND COMPANY

New York ❦ Boston

Also by Ruth Sanderson:

Cinderella
The Golden Mare, the Firebird, and the Magic Ring
The Crystal Mountain
Tapestries: Stories of Women in the Bible
Papa Gatto: An Italian Fairy Tale
The Twelve Dancing Princesses
The Night Before Christmas

Little, Brown and Company

Time Warner Book Group
1271 Avenue of the Americas, New York, NY 10020
Visit our Web site at www.lb-kids.com

First Edition

The Snow Princess was inspired by the Russian opera *The Snow Maiden*.

Library of Congress Cataloging-in-Publication Data

Sanderson, Ruth.
    The Snow Princess / written and illustrated by Ruth Sanderson—1st ed.
      p. cm.
    Summary: Despite the warnings of her parents, Father Frost and Mother Spring, the
Snow Princess falls in love with a human and risks losing her immortality.
    ISBN 0-316-77982-2
    [1. Fairy tales.] I. Title.

PZ8.S253 Sn 2004
[Fic]—dc21   2002040657

10 9 8 7 6 5 4 3 2 1

TWP

Book design by Tracy Shaw

Printed in Singapore

The illustrations for this book were done in oils.
The text was set in Post Antiqua, and the display type was hand-lettered.

For Maria,
who has helped me to shape ideas into words
and to craft words into story

Long ago and far away, Father Frost and Mother Spring had a daughter. They called her their Snow Princess because she could call up snowstorms at will. At first, she could create only small flurries. She loved to dance and spin as the snow swirled around her. As the Snow Princess grew older, she was able to call up mighty snowstorms.

In time, the little Snow Princess became a beautiful maiden who learned to use her power wisely. She begged her parents to let her leave their home in the icy north so that she might see more of the world. They agreed to let her go, with one warning.

"Remember this," Mother Spring said. "You must never fall in love."

"Yes," said Father Frost. "You are safe from death so long as love for a man does not enter your heart."

The Snow Princess shivered when she heard these words, but she longed to see the world, so she bid her parents good-bye.

The Snow Princess had many companions in her travels.
She crossed barren deserts of ice and snow with the polar bears.
Then she traveled south with herds of reindeer. In the great
forests, wolves padded silently by her side. At night, snowy
owls cast blue-black shadows as they glided above her in the
moonlight. But, as much as she loved all the animals, she longed
to see people and learn about their ways.

Eventually the Snow Princess reached the outskirts of a small village. She watched in fascination as two children built a snowman. Next to a cottage, a man with a red beard chopped wood, while a young man forked hay into a sheep pen. The young shepherd laughed when the two children threw snowballs at him. As the sun set and turned the snow to pale gold, a smiling woman opened the cottage door and called the family in for dinner.

For many days the Snow Princess watched from the forest as the family went about their daily routine. Sometimes the young man played on a flute and his little brother and sister danced in the snow. They all looked so merry.

One day, a group of people came by. They wore festive clothing, and some carried musical instruments.

"Come on, Sergei, we'll be late for the Festival," called one of them, and the young shepherd joined them, his flute in hand.

The Snow Princess followed in the woods as the group strolled along to the village. She was so interested in their laughing and chattering that she forgot to keep hidden.

It was Sergei who turned to her and said, "It would be much easier to walk on the path. Why don't you join us!" He stopped and offered her his hand.

The Snow Princess was terrified, but her curiosity was stronger than her fear. Taking his hand, she stepped out of the woods and onto the path. When he asked her name, she knew somehow that "Snow Princess" was not a proper human name. She had heard him call his little sister by the name of Katia, so she said, "Call me Katia."

At the Winter Festival, there were reindeer races, ice skating, and singing and dancing contests. Throughout the day, different musicians played for the dancers. Finally, Sergei and his friends played, and couples danced by the light of bonfires, until at last everyone was exhausted and could dance no more. Sergei went over to the Snow Princess and asked if he could walk her home.

How could she explain that the forest was her home, and the snow was her bed and blanket! When she shook her head, Sergei said, "Then I hope we will meet again soon."

That night the Snow Princess dreamed of her parents. Father Frost repeated his warning. "You are safe from death so long as love for a man does not enter your heart." She did not feel very safe. In the morning she did not go to watch Sergei tend the sheep, or to see his brother and sister playing in the snow. Instead, she walked northward into the wild woods and vowed to forget the world of humans.

The Snow Princess tried to amuse herself by spending time with the animals in the forest. She played with the foxes, chased the hares, and wandered with herds of deer. She called up snow flurries and tried to dance, but felt no joy in it.

As the weeks passed, the Snow Princess grew more and more unhappy. Finally, she could stand her solitude no longer. She turned back south toward the village, and she reached the cottage in a few days. Sergei was fixing a broken shutter, and she made up her mind to speak to him, for how could that cause harm! She invited him to take a walk with her. "It would be my pleasure, Katia," he said. The Snow Princess smiled. She liked having a real name.

When they reached a clearing, Katia paused and said, "Would you play your flute for me?"

As Sergei played for Katia, she felt a warmth she had never experienced.

And so, the Snow Princess and the shepherd became friends, and she looked forward to seeing him every day. The long winter months passed quickly, and in her happiness Katia forgot her parents' warning.

One night Katia had a terrible dream. In it, Father Frost was angry. "I tell you again, you are safe from death so long as love for a man does not enter your heart." As he spoke, he sent an ice storm to freeze her heart.

The Snow Princess awoke with a start; she did not want to die. She must try to freeze her heart, like her father did in her dream, so that love could not enter. She summoned a snowstorm and for a time forgot herself in the fury of the wind and snow.

"My heart is cold," she told herself as she huddled against the base of a huge tree. She let the storm rage on for the whole night, feeling cold to the bone.

In the morning she awoke to the sound of voices calling Sergei's name. She heard one man tell another that Sergei had gotten lost in the storm trying to find a sheep that had escaped its pen. Although the sheep had found its way home, Sergei himself was still missing. They were starting a search party to find him.

Katia rushed to join the search. As the hours passed with no sign of the shepherd, her worry deepened. The Snow Princess began to feel a strange warmth in her heart. The snow started to melt as well, as if in sympathy with her feelings.

If I die, so be it, the Snow Princess thought to herself. *Just let me find him first*, she prayed. Her heart grew warmer. The snow continued to melt.

The Snow Princess searched and searched. At long last the melting snow revealed her love, half-buried and unconscious. He must have tripped over a root in the dark and fallen.

"Sergei, wake up. Please wake up, Sergei!" she cried as she knelt beside him.

"Ah, my Snow Princess," he said, opening his eyes. "Am I dreaming? Or have I died and this is heaven?"

"It is I who will die soon," said Katia. "For I am the daughter of Father Frost and Mother Spring, and they told me I would die if I fell in love."

She touched the cheek of the shepherd, and suddenly her fingers felt warm. Her face was no longer pale but had a healthy pink glow. As a matter of fact, she felt quite wonderful, not in the least like she was dying.

As the snow continued to melt, the bare patches of earth began to send up shoots and leaves and buds. Katia watched in amazement. Then she saw her mother, Spring, standing amidst the new growth.

"I love a man and I have not died yet," said Katia to her mother.

"You will die surely enough, my daughter," said Mother Spring, "for love has touched your heart. Now you are human and mortal, and like all mortals, you will grow old and die." After she spoke, Mother Spring slowly faded from Katia's sight.

"Who were you talking to?" asked Sergei. "I thought I heard a voice, but I didn't see anyone there."

Katia smiled and helped him to his feet. "It was no one," she said. "Just a spring breeze waking the earth from its long winter sleep."

Then Katia and Sergei walked hand in hand out of the forest, into the warm sunshine of a perfect spring day.